Chip and Wilf were tracking Dad.
"This is a good game," said Wilf.

1

"Put this in your hat," said Chip. "Dad won't see us. Then we can track him."

Chip and Wilf hid in the trees.
"Keep down," said Chip. "Here comes
Dad."

Dad went past. He looked for the
boys, but he couldn't see them.

Floppy went sniff, sniff, sniff!
"Go away, Floppy!" said Chip, but
Floppy wouldn't go.

The magic took them to Africa. Some
zebra were going to drink at a pool.

Chip and Wilf looked around.
"A herd of zebra!" said Wilf. "Don't
let them see us!"

"Oh no!" said Wilf. "They are going
to catch a zebra."

"We must stop them," said Chip. He
had an idea.
"Come on," he said.

The boys ran to the lorry. Chip
pressed the horn.
"Beeeeeeeep!" it went.

"Beeeeeeeep!" went the horn again.
The zebra looked up.

The men couldn't start the lorry.
Suddenly a jeep drove up. There were
rangers in the jeep.

The men jumped out of the lorry and ran away. The rangers chased after them.

A ranger shook Chip's hand.
"Thank you," he said. "You saved a
zebra."

The magic key began to glow. It was time to go. It had been an exciting adventure.

"Why wouldn't the lorry start?"
asked Wilf.

"Ha! I took the key!" said Chip.